tiny titans

and the
science Fa[...]

by Art
Baltazar

GROSSET & DUNLAP
AN IMPRINT OF PENGUIN GROUP (USA) INC.

GROSSET & DUNLAP
Published by the Penguin Group
Penguin Group (USA) Inc., 375 Hudson Street, New York, New York 10014, USA
Penguin Group (Canada), 90 Eglinton Avenue East, Suite 700, Toronto, Ontario M4P 2Y3, Canada
(a division of Pearson Penguin Canada Inc.)
Penguin Books Ltd., 80 Strand, London WC2R 0RL, England
Penguin Group Ireland, 25 St. Stephen's Green, Dublin 2, Ireland
(a division of Penguin Books Ltd.)
Penguin Group (Australia), 250 Camberwell Road, Camberwell, Victoria 3124,
Australia (a division of Pearson Australia Group Pty. Ltd.)
Penguin Books India Pvt. Ltd., 11 Community Centre, Panchsheel Park, New Delhi—110 017, India
Penguin Group (NZ), 67 Apollo Drive, Rosedale, North Shore 0632, New Zealand
(a division of Pearson New Zealand Ltd.)
Penguin Books (South Africa) (Pty.) Ltd., 24 Sturdee Avenue, Rosebank,
Johannesburg 2196, South Africa

Penguin Books Ltd., Registered Offices: 80 Strand, London WC2R 0RL, England

Published by Grosset & Dunlap, a division of Penguin Young Readers Group,
345 Hudson Street, New York, New York 10014. GROSSET & DUNLAP
is a trademark of Penguin Group (USA) Inc. Printed in the U.S.A.

Library of Congress Control Number: 2009020849

ISBN 978-0-448-45248-7   10 9 8 7 6 5 4 3 2 1

Meet the ... tiny titans

STARFIRE

ROBIN

CYBORG

She's an alien princess. Very naive and free-spirited. She finds the good in others. Has a crush on Robin and thinks he's cute, but so do all the other girls.

(Dick Grayson) The brave and serious leader of the Tiny Titans. Although he is the original Robin, he is very moody. Also, he has secret crushes on Starfire and Barbara Gordon.

Half boy, half robot. Cyborg is always tinkering with mechanical gadgets, often turning them into something else. His battle cry "BOO-YA!" has earned him the nickname "Big Boo-Ya."

BARBARA GORDON

Daughter of Police Commissioner Gordon. Barbara has a secret Batcave hidden behind her bedroom wall where she keeps her Bat-Tricyle. She has a crush on Robin and his yellow cape.

WONDER GIRL

(Donna) Raised by Amazons. She's strong and cute. Never lie to her—she has a magical jump rope which makes people tell the truth. Very skeptical.

AQUALAD

The little boy from the ocean. Has a pet fish named Fluffy. Aqualad can communicate with all forms of sea life.

TERRA

The sometimes-hated little girl who likes to throw rocks. Principal Slade's teacher's pet. She thinks Beast Boy is a weirdo.

BEAST BOY

The green little boy who can change into any animal he desires. He's a prankster and loves comics. Has a crush on Terra.

BUMBLEBEE

The tiniest of the Tiny Titans. Bumblebee buzzes and packs a mighty stinger.

chapter one

It was a bright, sunny morning and the Tiny Titans, students at Sidekick City Elementary, scrambled to take their seats in the classroom.

The school's science fair was coming up in two weeks and their teacher hoped everyone was working on their projects.

Robin, the Boy Wonder, looked over at the other Titans. "Aw, man," he said. "The science fair is in two weeks. I gotta start something!"

"I've already started mine!" Cyborg said with a proud smile. "I'm building a robot that will help me take out the trash!"

"Oh yeah!" Aqualad jumped up. "I'm making a chart of underwater sea life!"

"Well, I'm going to build a mini-universe," Starfire said excitedly. "And it will include my home planet of Tamaran!"

She looked over at Beast Boy sitting quietly at his desk. He wasn't being his usual troublemaking self. "So," she asked, "what are you making?"

Beast Boy didn't seem to hear what Starfire was saying. He was too busy looking at the little girl sitting at the desk next to him. Her name was Terra and she liked to play with rocks.

Terra turned to Beast Boy and gave him a weird look. "Leave me alone!" she shouted. "Stop bothering me!"

CLUNK!

Before Beast Boy could look away, Terra picked up a rock and threw it at him.

"Ow!" Beast Boy cried as he held his head.

Dr. Light interrupted. "Remember, you only have two weeks to finish your science projects! That goes for you, too, Beast Boy!"

chapter TWO

Later that afternoon, Cyborg and Beast Boy walked home from school.

"Hey, Beast Boy," Cyborg asked, "do you know what you're going to make for your science project?"

"Oh, Terra," Beast Boy sighed in a haze.

"Terra?!" Cyborg exclaimed. "Terra's not a science project!"

"No, here comes Terra!" Beast Boy yelled.

Beast Boy quickly leaped into a rosebush. He poked his head out as Terra walked by, surprising her and almost knocking her over.

"AAHHH!" screamed Terra. "What's wrong with you, Beast Boy? You're not supposed to frighten girls like that!"

"Hello, Terra! Here, this rose is for you!" said Beast Boy. "Doesn't it smell lovely?"

Terra leaned closer to the flower and, with a big sniff, started to sneeze.

"AHHHH CHOOOO!!!"

"Um, sorry, Terra. I didn't know you were allergic," said Beast Boy. "Here, hold the rose while I get you a tissue," he said.

"OW!" screamed Terra. "There are thorns on this flower! What are you trying to do to me? I hope you have some bandages with those tissues, you jerk!"

Terra pushed Beast Boy into the rosebush and angrily walked away.

Cyborg, who had witnessed the whole thing, looked at Beast Boy lying in the bush and said, "Just face it, loverboy. Sometimes love hurts."

Chapter Three

"Oh boy, I can't wait to work on my robot today! I LOVE SATURDAYS!" Cyborg shouted as he leaped out of bed.

He ate a bowl of cereal and then ran to the Titans' tree house. Just as he grabbed a wrench, he heard the secret knock at the tree house door:

KNOCKITY, KNOCK, KNOCK!

"Who is it?" Cyborg called out.

"It's me, Robin!" the Boy Wonder said as he walked into the tree house.

"You're just in time to see my new robot in action! I call him FELIX!" Cyborg said. "FELIX stands for Fantastic, Excellent, Logistic, Intelligent, X-treme!"

Cyborg hit a few buttons on his remote control, and a lightbulb at the top of FELIX's antenna lit up. The robot rolled over to the closet, grabbed a dustpan and shovel, and began to sweep the tree house floor.

"See, I programmed him to do all my chores," Cyborg said with a smile. "FELIX, I'm a little hungry. Would you make Robin and me some sandwiches?"

The lightbulb in FELIX's antenna lit up again. He immediately stopped his cleaning duties and made some sandwiches.

After making the sandwiches, FELIX mopped the floor, cleaned the windows, watered the plants, picked up all the trash, and took it outside!

Cyborg and Robin chased after FELIX. They ran out to the street where they saw Beast Boy following Terra.

"Oh, Terra, your hair smells so divine," Beast Boy said as he pressed his nose against the back of Terra's head.

SNIFF! SNIFF!

"Would you stop smelling me?" Terra shouted. "Leave me alone, you FREAK!!"

FELIX, who was still in garbage-cleaning mode, picked Beast Boy up and tossed him into the trash can.

"Well, at least you didn't get hit with rocks this time," said Cyborg.

Chapter Four

Later that day, Robin was in the Batcave working on his science fair project. Barbara Gordon happily rode her Bat-Tricycle around to see what the Boy Wonder was doing.

"Hi, Robin," she said as she sped by. "What are you working on?"

"I'm making the ultimate crime-fighting Utility Belt!" Robin said proudly. "It holds more gadgets than you can imagine!"

"Really? That sounds exciting!" Barbara said. "Does it have a Batrope?"

"Of course it does." Robin nodded.

"Does it have a Bat-Telescope and a Batarang?" asked Barbara.

"Sure does," replied the Boy Wonder. "It has all kinds of Bat-Stuff."

"Does it have an ice cream scooper? Or a garden hose? Or a hammer?" Barbara continued to ask.

"Yep, yep, yep," said Robin.

"A hot dog maker?" asked Barbara.

"Yep," said Robin.

"A pogo stick?" asked Barbara.

"Two of them," replied Robin.

Suddenly, Robin's Utility Belt began ringing.
RING, RING! RING, RING!
"Oh, it's the Bat-Phone," Robin said.

"Yes, Commissioner," Robin spoke into the phone. "Yes, it's me, Robin. Batman? No, he's not here, sir. Can I take a message? Okay, I'll let him know. What? Oh, yeah, she's here. Okay, I'll tell her. Okay. Bye."

"It was your dad," Robin said to Barbara.
"He said to go home. It's dinnertime."

"What are we having?" Barbara asked.

"Macaroni and cheese," Robin said.

"WOO-HOO!" Barbara shouted
with glee.

"I wonder if my Utility Belt has voicemail,
too," said Robin.

Chapter Five

Meanwhile, back at the Titans' tree house, Starfire was assembling her mini-universe science project.

"Here's the paint you wanted, Starfire!" said Bumblebee as she flew in through the door.

"Cool," Starfire said. "Right in time, too. I just ran out of red."

Starfire opened the red paint, dipped in her brush, and painted the finishing touches on her tiny planets.

"There we go." Starfire smiled. "All finished! An exact mini-replica of the universe."

"Starfire," Bumblebee asked. "Do you think there is life on any of the other planets?"

Just then, the girls were startled by the sound of thunder rumbling across the sky.

RUMBLE RUMBLE RUMBLE!

"Life on other planets?" Starfire said as she looked out the door of the tree house. "Yep, and I think they've just arrived."

The door of the spacecraft opened and in the doorway stood several small, pointy-eared, green alien visitors.

"Greetings, Earth creatures!" said the alien leader. "We were searching the cosmos for other intelligent life and were strangely drawn to your mini-replica of our home world."

"These aliens look just like Beast Boy!" Starfire whispered to Bumblebee. "They have the same green skin and pointy ears."

"As a gift," the alien leader said as he handed a bunch of rocks to Starfire, "we would like to give you these meteorites from our home planet."

"Farewell, young earthlings," said the alien.
"And good luck on your science fair project."

"Thank you, Mr. Alien, sir," Starfire said.

"I think Terra could really use these rocks," Starfire told Bumblebee.

"She's just going to throw them at Beast Boy, you know," Bumblebee replied.

Chapter Six

aves crashed upon the sandy beach as Beast Boy ran along the shore. He transformed into a fish and swam to the deepest part of the sea so he could visit his friend, Aqualad.

"Hi, Aqualad," Beast Boy said. "What are you doing?"

"Working on my science project," Aqualad replied. "It's a chart all about the evolution of sea life."

"I know it's about sea life, but why are you working on it underwater?" Beast Boy asked.

"The ocean helps me think better," Aqualad said. "How about you? Do you like being able to transform into a fish for a day?"

"I love it!" Beast Boy said as he wiggled his fins. "I get to swim around without a care in the world, visit my underwater sea horse friends, and it gives me a break from Terra throwing rocks at my head."

"I thought you liked when she did that," Aqualad said.

"I do, and I think she likes throwing them at me, too," Beast Boy said. "In fact, she just threw some rocks at me. I think they were meteorites from outer space."

"Really?" Aqualad asked.

"Yep. Terra said Starfire gave them to her."

"That's so cool," Aqualad said sadly.

Beast Boy looked at Aqualad and noticed he seemed a little unhappy.

"What's wrong?" asked Beast Boy.

"I wish a girl would throw rocks at my head," Aqualad replied.

"Really?" Beast Boy said excitedly. "Well, I'll ask around. Maybe Terra has a sister."

chapter Seven

"Good morning, students!" said Dr. Light. "Who would like to show their project first?"

A moan swept across the classroom.

"I'll go first!" Cyborg shouted. "My science project is a robot named FELIX. I programmed him to help me with my chores!"

Cyborg pressed a button on the remote and FELIX began cleaning the classroom.

He swept the floor, threw out the trash,
and even clapped the chalkboard erasers.

"Who's next?" Dr. Light said, coughing
through a chalky dust cloud.

Robin jumped up in front of the classroom
and said, "My science project is the ultimate
crime-fighting Utility Belt. Allow me to
demonstrate."

Robin began to take lots of different things out of his Utility Belt. He took out a Batrope, Bat-Screwdriver, Bat-Mug, Bat-Hammer, Bat-Fishing pole, Bat-Thermos, Bat-Fork, Bat-Iron, Bat-Football, Bat-Baseball bat, Bat-Shovel, and Bat-Refrigerator.

"*OKAY!* We get it!" Dr. Light interrupted. "Your ultimate Utility Belt holds lots of things."

Next up was Beast Boy.

"What will you demonstrate for us today?" asked Dr. Light.

"I built a model of Sidekick City's very own mountain range, sir. And as you can see, I used different layers of rock," said Beast Boy. "I even included some meteorites from outer space."

"Wow, Beast Boy, that sure is a fascinating collection of rocks you have there," Dr. Light said.

Beast Boy sat in his chair and leaned back with his hands behind his head.

Suddenly the little girl Terra turned to Beast Boy and said curiously, "Wow, Beast Boy, I didn't know that you liked rocks, too!"

The End!

maze

Help Beast Boy reach Terra
through the rock maze.